THE ICE CREAM KING

GREG McEVOY

Stoddart
Kids

TORONTO • NEW YORK

*We acknowledge the Canada Council for the Arts and the
Ontario Arts Council for their support of our publishing program.*

Published in Canada in 1998 by
Stoddart Kids,
a division of Stoddart Publishing Co. Limited
34 Lesmill Road
Toronto, Canada M3B 2T6
Tel (416) 445-3333 Fax (416) 445-5967
E-mail Customer.Service@ccmailgw.genpub.com

Published in the United States in 1998 by
Stoddart Kids
a division of Stoddart Publishing Co. Limited
180 Varick Street, 9th Floor
New York, New York 14207
Toll free 1-800-805-1083
E-mail gdsinc@genpub.com

Distributed in Canada by
General Distribution Services
30 Lesmill Road
Toronto, Canada M3B 2T6
Tel (416) 445-3333 Fax (416) 445-5967
E-mail Customer.Service@ccmailgw.genpub.com

Distributed in the United States by
General Distribution Services
85 River Rock Drive, Suite 202
Buffalo, New York 14207
Toll free 1-800-805-1083
E-mail gdsinc@genpub.com

Canadian Cataloguing in Publication Data

McEvoy, Greg
Ice cream king

ISBN 0-7737-3069-9

I. Title.

PS8575.E86I23 1998   jC813'.54   C97-931857-2
PZ7.M34Ic 1998

Printed and bound in Hong Kong, China by
Book Art Inc., Toronto

For my brother, Glenn

Even when he was very young, Lionel knew two things for certain.
One was that he had a terrible weakness for ice cream.
Every Saturday afternoon an old horse-drawn wagon rolled past his house.
"Ice cream! Getcher ice cream!" the driver would call.
It was Lionel's favorite day of the week.
The other thing was this. If he was going to grow up and work for a living,
he might as well have the best job possible. It seemed to him that kings
were pretty well paid and powerful people. Besides, he was sure they could
have all the ice cream they wanted. Yes, being a king would be perfect.

His dog, Prince, was in complete agreement. Lionel and
Prince would lie in bed for hours discussing the best way to run
a kingdom. Then, late one night, they saw something amazing
advertised on television — King School. Lionel pleaded with his
parents to enroll him. It took a long time, but finally they agreed.

The night before he was to leave for King School, Lionel lay awake thinking how he could change the world once he was king. There would be no more wars, or pollution, or unemployment, or crime. But there would be ice cream — and lots of it — for everybody.

In the morning, Lionel's family drove him to the train station. His father was giving him some last minute advice when the conductor yelled, "All aboooooard!" Lionel's mother tried not to cry, but she couldn't help it.

Everyone hugged Lionel as he boarded the train.

"Don't forget to write to us," his father shouted as the train pulled away.

"I won't," Lionel yelled back.

"And don't eat too much ice cream!"

Lionel heard his mother call out to him, but he pretended he didn't.

The King School was magnificent. Lionel stood at the huge front gates and stared. It was the most exciting moment of his young life. For the next year this would be his home.

Hundreds of other princely little boys had come from all over the world, eager to begin their studies. After signing in at the front desk, they were shown to their rooms.

Once everyone was settled, classes began. The students were instructed in the many rules of royalty. They learned how to give speeches and royal decrees, how to sit up properly on their thrones, how to avoid tripping over red carpets, and how to keep their crowns on straight.

There was history about the lives of famous kings. There was a class on manners and how to invite important people to a royal ball. There were books to read and exams to pass.

Lionel studied as hard as he could and all the while he
imagined what it would be like to have his own little kingdom.
His long hours in the library were rewarded. He earned very high
marks in all his subjects. Finally, the year was over and school
was finished.

On graduation day there was a huge banquet for the students and their families. After dessert — the best ice cream he had ever tasted — Lionel was called to the stage to receive his diploma. It read:

*This is to certify that **Lionel** has completed
all the courses at King School and is therefore qualified
for a full time position as King.*

The students gave their teachers a standing ovation.

Then it was time to go home.

The next evening Lionel began searching for the job of his dreams. He read the newspaper for "King Wanted" ads, but there were none. He looked in the yellow pages under castles, but there didn't seem to be any. So he got out his map and studied it. Just when he was beginning to feel frustrated, Lionel noticed a building on the lower right hand corner. The printing beside it read "Royal Palace."

"Finally!" Lionel shouted. "I will apply to be king in the morning."

After a good night's sleep and a bowlful of ice cream Lionel
grabbed his diploma, put on his best crown, called a taxi, kissed
his mom, whistled for Prince, and headed out the door.

The palace was everything Lionel could have wished for. The walls and towers were solid marble and the spires were polished copper. A deep moat of sparkling water surrounded it, but the heavy drawbridge was down as if to welcome Lionel in. An enormous watchman stood guard at the front gate. Without further delay, Lionel rushed forward to speak with him.

"Good morning," Lionel said in his most regal voice. "I am here to apply for the job of king. As you can see, I'm very well qualified."

The guard stared down at him. Slowly he shook his head. "My dear boy," he began in a very discouraging tone of voice. "You cannot *apply* to be king."

"I can't?" Lionel asked, swallowing hard.

"Of course not," the guard continued. "That isn't how it works. It's all in the family, you see. When His Majesty retires, his oldest son will take over. Then, when *he* retires, *his* oldest child will become king or queen. When *that* king or queen retires..."

"OK, OK!" Lionel interrupted. "I get the idea." He looked around, trying to think. "Fine then," he said. "Could you please tell me the way to the next royal palace so I can apply *there* to be king?"

"My dear boy," said the watchman in that voice again, "there is only *one* royal palace and only *one* king!"

There was a moment of silence so silent that Lionel could hear his own heart beating. A look of horror crept slowly across his face. In a very high voice he said, "Thank you." Then he walked back across the bridge in a daze.

Lionel walked until he came to a telephone booth. It gave him an idea. He would call King School and get this whole mess straightened out. He dialed the number.

"We're sorry, the number you have called is no longer in service," said a recorded message.

Lionel dropped the receiver. "No…longer…in…service…" he sputtered. He felt weak. He had to sit down. For a moment Lionel thought he was going to faint. Then, off in the distance he heard something familiar.

"Ice cream! Getcher ice cream right here!"

Lionel looked up. A horse-drawn wagon was coming down the road. It bumped to a stop in front of Lionel.

"Good afternoon, Yer Majesty," chirped the driver. Then he peered down at Lionel. "Aren't you a long way from home?"

"I'm not a king," Lionel answered.

"It doesn't look like I ever will be either. And as far as home goes, I don't even have the taxi fare to get back." Then he explained his entire story about the school, his dream of being king, and his big disappointment at the castle.

"Well," said the ice cream man cheerfully. "I happen to be looking for someone to help me run my ice cream wagon."

"But I'm not qualified," moaned Lionel. "I don't have any experience. I don't know how to do anything except be a king."

"Well, can you shout, 'Ice cream! Getcher ice cream!'?"

"Sure," answered Lionel.

"Then you've got the job! Besides, I've always wanted a fancier name for my business. Now that I have a new partner... how does *The Ice Cream King* sound to you?"

"*The Ice Cream King*," Lionel whispered in awe.

"Sounds a lot better than plain old *Ice Cream*, doesn't it?"
Lionel had to agree.

"Then welcome aboard!" The ice cream man held out his hand
and pulled his new partner up into the wagon. As they drove
towards his house, Lionel began to grin.

"Ice cream! Getcher ice cream!" Lionel shouted.
"Today's special is Rrrroyal Rrrripple, twenty-five cents a scoop!"

Lionel felt just like a king.